First U.S. edition 2015 • Library of Congress Catalog Card Number 2014951790 • ISBN 978-0-7636-7834-0 • This book was typeset in Futura • The illustrations were done in watercolor • Candlewick Press, 99 Dover Street, Somerville, Massachusetts 02144 • visit us at www.candlewick.com • Printed in Humen, Dongguan, China

15 16 17 18 19 20 SCP 10 9 8 7 6 5 4 3 2 1

THE SEEDS OF FRIENDSHIP

MICHAEL FOREMAN

CANDLEWICK PRESS

Adam loved his new home.

It was high, high in a tall tower in the city.

It was exciting. He was living in the sky.

But Adam missed
the faraway place
where he used to
live. Every evening
he asked his mom
and dad to read him
stories that brought
back memories of
their old home.

Adam drew pictures
to go with the stories
and pinned them on
his bedroom wall.

But when he looked from
his bedroom window, he
saw a very different picture.
He saw a cold, gray world.

It seemed so empty, too.

Sometimes he saw children

playing far below in the shadows of the buildings,

but he was too shy to go down and say hello.

Then one morning Adam couldn't see out of his window at all. The glass was frosted over, and the icy patterns reminded Adam of a frozen forest.

With his finger, Adam drew animals to live there.

When his window-forest was full, he ran to the next window, and the next and the next, until every one was full.

That night, Adam saw

snow for the first time.

In the morning, the dark, gray world was gone.

It was a white wonderland! Adam rushed

downstairs and out into the snow. It was so cold!

Some children were

building a snowman.

Adam touched the snow. It was light and wet and cold all at once. He started to build a snow elephant.

"That's a bit small for an elephant!" one of the children said with a laugh. "Let's make a big one." Then they threw a snowball at him. Adam laughed.

So they all worked together to build

the biggest elephant they could.

When they had finished, Adam started to make a snow hippo.

The other children copied him, and soon there were snow rhinos

and lions, a snow crocodile,

and a snow camel, too.

By supper time, the

snowman was in charge

of a whole snow zoo!

A few days later, when the snowy world had melted,

it was time for Adam to start at his new school.

He was pleased to see that some of his new friends

were there. They showed him around. Adam's favorite

place was a small garden. It was a wonderful splash

of green in the gray playground.

Adam's teacher gave him some seeds from the

garden to take home. He gave them to his mom.

He didn't know what kind of seeds they were,

but his mom planted them in the window boxes.

"Let's see what happens," she said.

As the months passed, the school's garden grew and Adam brought more plants and seeds home. Once the window boxes were full, Adam and his friends found tin cans and pots and pans and carried them up to the roof. Together they made a garden in the sky.

"Let's make more gardens!" said the children.

So Adam and his friends made gardens on

any empty patch of ground they could find.

Now Adam no longer sees a gray world.

He sees a city of gardens.